MY BOOK OF MORMON STORYBOOK
IS PRESENTED TO:

_____

ON THIS DATE:

_____

PRESENTED BY:

_____

Author's Note: This book contains quotes from the Book of Mormon. They are characterized in *italic* print. Quotes not in italic print are used for continuity of the story line. Also, because this storybook is written for young children, some stories have purposely excluded violent content.

ISBN: 1-55517-352-7

10 9 8 7 6 5

Published and Distributed by:

925 North Main, Springville, UT 84663 • 801/489-4084

CFI Publishing and Distribution Since 1986

Cedar Fort, Incorporated

CFI Distribution • CFI Books • Inside Cougar Report

Typeset and Page Layout by Corinne A. Bischoff
Printed in the United States of America

For Amanda, Ryan and Sean

Thank you for showing me the need for this type of storybook with lots of bright and colorful pictures. You were my constant inspiration as I tried to see the world through your eyes. May your curiosity, creativity and faith in God stay with you throughout your life and may you always know how much I love you!

My
Book of Mormon
Storybook

90 Favorite Stories

As Told and Illustrated by Laura Lee Rostrom

CONTENTS

LEHI'S VISION

A long time ago lived a man named Lehi. Lehi was a good man. He always prayed to Heavenly Father. Because of his faith in God, he saw many visions.

In one of his visions, he saw the city
of Jerusalem being destroyed. God
told Lehi to warn all the people who
lived in the city. But the people would
not listen to him. They did not
believe their great city could be
destroyed. Some people were angry
with Lehi.

Some people wanted to kill Lehi
because they did not like his visions.
But because Lehi was following the
Lord's commandments, he and his
family were not harmed.

1 Nephi 1

THE WILDERNESS

Lehi and his wife Sariah and their family left their home and wealth behind in Jerusalem. The Lord told them to flee into the wilderness. Laman and Lemuel were Lehi's oldest sons. They did not want to leave their home in Jerusalem. They murmured against their father.

Nephi and Sam were also Lehi's
sons. But they believed their father's
prophesies and they wanted to follow
the Lord's commandments. This
made Lehi happy.

1 Nephi 2

THE BRASS PLATES

While in the wilderness, Lehi had another vision. Laban, the ruler of Jerusalem, had important records on brass plates. The Lord wanted Lehi to have them.

So Lehi asked his four sons to return to Jerusalem. Lehi told them to get the brass plates from Laban. His sons were discouraged. They did not know how to get the brass plates from Laban. But the Lord helped them.

1 Nephi 4

GETTING THE BRASS PLATES

When Nephi and his brothers returned to Jerusalem they needed a plan to get the brass plates. They decided that one person would go talk to Laban and ask for the brass plates. They cast lots to see who would go. It was Laman.

Laman walked to Laban's house and asked for the brass plates. This made Laban angry. He called Laman a robber and threw him out. Laman felt scared and discouraged. He returned to his brothers and told them what happened.

Now they needed a new plan. They
left all of their gold and silver and
nice things behind in Jerusalem.
Maybe Laban would let them buy the
brass plates with their gold and silver.

When Laban saw all of their gold and
silver, he wanted it for himself. But he
did not want to give them the brass
plates in return.

So Laban ordered his servants to slay Nephi and his brothers. Nephi and his brothers ran away. They found a big rock to hide inside. They were safe from Laban now.

1 Nephi 3

AN ANGEL'S VISIT

After losing their gold and silver and after being thrown out of Laban's house twice, Laman was feeling angry. He was angry with his father Lehi for asking him to get the brass plates. He was also angry at Nephi for wanting to obey their father.

Laman and Lemuel started fighting
with Nephi and Sam. They were
even hitting them. Laman had a rod
and was about to hit Nephi when
something incredible happened.

An angel appeared. The angel told
Laman and Lemuel to stop hurting
Nephi and Sam. The angel told them
to go into Jerusalem one more time.

1 Nephi 3

NEPHI'S FAITH

Nephi did not know how to get the brass plates. But he had faith. He knew the Lord would help him. When Nephi came to Laban's house, it was night time. Nephi found Laban lying on the ground in a deep sleep. Nephi was surprised! He wondered why Laban was sleeping outside all alone. Nephi took off Laban's clothes and sword. He put them on himself.

Now Nephi looked like Laban
because he was wearing Laban's
clothes and sword. Looking like
Laban, Nephi entered Laban's house.
He asked to see the brass plates. He
took the plates back to his brothers.
When they saw him coming, they
thought it was Laban coming to slay
them. They were frightened.

But it was just Nephi wearing Laban's clothes. They were glad when they saw it was really Nephi. All the brothers were very happy now. The Lord did help them to get the brass plates.

1 Nephi 4

SARIAH'S CONCERNS

Nephi and his brothers were far away from home while getting the brass plates. Their mother was very worried about them. She was frightened something bad might happen to them. She was angry that Lehi asked them to go back to Jerusalem. She complained to Lehi.

But Lehi said, "The Lord wants them
to go and He will protect them." After
a while, Nephi and his brothers did
come home safely. They had the
brass plates, too.

Sariah was happy. Now she knew the
Lord protected and helped her sons.
They were glad to be back together.

1 Nephi 5

THE LIAHONA

The Lord wanted Lehi and his family to go on a journey. But they were in a big wilderness. Lehi did not know where to go. One day Lehi found something at his front door.

He found a round ball. It was made
of brass. There were two spindles on
it. This special brass ball directed
them where to go. Lehi called this
brass ball, the Liahona.

1 Nephi 16, Alma 37:38

BUILDING A SHIP

After eight years in the wilderness, Lehi and his family came to a land by the sea. They called it Bountiful because of its richness in fruits and honey. Here, the Lord asked Nephi to build a ship. They would sail to a promised land.

Nephi did not have tools to build a ship. He did not even know how to build a ship. But the Lord told him where to find ore to make tools. And the Lord told him how to build a special ship.

1 Nephi 17

FINDING HELP

Nephi needed help building the
ship. He asked Laman and Lemuel
for help. But they would not help
him. They just laughed at him.

They said Nephi did not know how to build a ship and it was too much work. This made Nephi sad. He could not build the ship alone. It made Laman and Lemuel happy to see Nephi sad.

They called Nephi a fool for wanting
to build a ship. So Nephi told them it
was God who wanted them to build a
ship. He said, "If God can do great
miracles, like turning a sea into dry
land for Moses, then he can teach me
how to build a ship."

Laman and Lemuel did not like listening to their younger brother. They decided to throw Nephi into the sea. But Nephi was filled with the power of God and said, *"I command you that ye touch me not."* For many days, Laman and Lemuel could not touch Nephi.

Later on, the Lord told Nephi to touch
Laman and Lemuel. He would give
them a big shock. By this shock, they
would know that God needs them to
help build this ship. Nephi touched
Laman and Lemuel and gave them a
big shock.

From this powerful shock, Laman and
Lemuel finally knew that God wanted
them to help Nephi. Together, Nephi
and all his brothers built a fine ship.

1 Nephi 17, (1 Nephi 17:48)

ON THE SHIP

All of Lehi's family boarded the ship. They were going to sail to the promised land. The Liahona showed them where to go.

While on the ship, Laman and Lemuel
started getting loud and rude. Nephi
asked them to stop. They were
bothering the young children on board.
They were bothering their parents too.
But Laman and Lemuel would not stop.

They tied Nephi up with a cord.
Now they could do anything they
wanted. Nephi started to worry. The
Liahona only worked when they
were righteous. They would not
know where to go if the Liahona
stopped working.

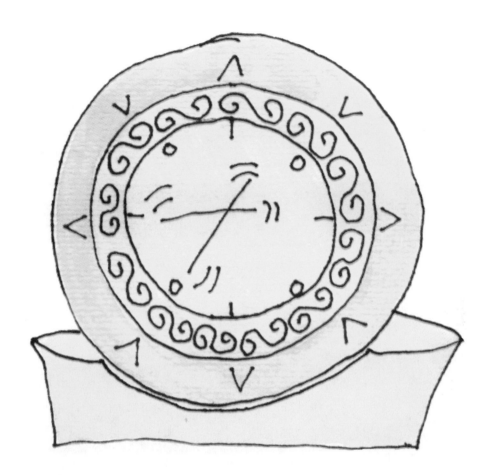

Now that Nephi was tied up and Laman and Lemuel were running the ship, Nephi thought the Liahona would stop directing them. Nephi was right. The Liahona stopped working.

1 Nephi 18

A BIG STORM

Laman and Lemuel refused to
untie Nephi. Even after three days,
they still refused to let Nephi go. And
the Liahona had stopped directing
them too. So for three days, they did
not know where to sail the ship.

Then a big storm came. There were
big gusts of wind and lots of rain. At
first, the storm did not scare Laman
and Lemuel. But on the fourth day,
something changed. Laman and
Lemuel could not control the ship. The
storm was so strong, they thought they
might be swallowed up in the ocean.
They thought they might die.

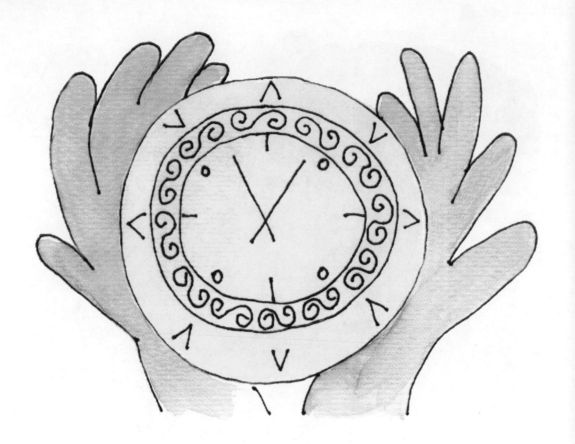

Finally, they untied Nephi. Nephi
praised the Lord. He prayed to God
asking for the storm to stop. Because
Nephi was righteous, the storm
stopped and the Liahona started
working again. It led them to the
Promised Land.

1 Nephi 18

THE PROMISED LAND

Lehi and his family were very happy. They arrived in the Promised Land. Lehi had a vision. He saw Jerusalem being destroyed after they left. Had they stayed in Jerusalem, they would have died.

They were grateful that God told them to leave. They were glad that God brought them to the Promised Land. They could live happy and free in the Promised Land.

LEHI'S LAST DAYS

Lehi was getting very old now. Before he died, he talked to his family. He said the Lord is pleased with people who follow His commandments. He will bless righteous people. They will have all that they need.

But God is not happy with people
who disobey. He cannot protect
wicked people. They may have wars.
They may live in fear.

Lehi blessed his family. He asked
them to follow God's commandments.
He prayed for peace in the Promised
Land.

2 Nephi 1-4

THE LAND OF NEPHI

With the Lord's help, Nephi became a teacher and a leader. This made Laman and Lemuel angry. They did not like their younger brother telling them what to do. They decided to kill Nephi once and for all.

The Lord told Nephi their plan. He
told Nephi to flee into the wilderness.
Nephi took his wife and children. His
brothers, Sam, Jacob and Joseph,
went also. So did his sisters.

They took the brass plates and the
Liahona with them. They traveled in
the wilderness for many, many days.
They called their new home Nephi.

THE NEPHITES

In the Land of Nephi, the people
called themselves Nephites. They
asked Nephi to be their king. Nephi
did not want the people to have a
king. But finally they persuaded him
to be their king and teacher. He
taught them to work hard, to plant
seeds for food and to build buildings.
He taught them about God. They built
a beautiful temple. They began to
have all that they needed.

2 Nephi 5

THE LAMANITES

The people who stayed with Laman and Lemuel called themselves Lamanites. They did not remember the Lord. They did not follow His commandments. The Lord made the skin of the Lamanites a different color. The Nephites would know the Lamanites by their dark skin.

They would know the Lamanites did
not remember God. The Lamanites
did not work hard. They did not plant
food. They only hunted wild animals
for meat to eat. Sometimes they were
hungry. They did not always have
what they needed.

2 Nephi 5

JACOB TELLS OF JESUS

Nephi's brother, Jacob, became very wise. He taught the Nephites many things. He told them about Jesus. He said Jesus would be born on earth. Jesus would refuse evil and choose good things. He would teach people how to be happy.

Jesus would die but live again. These
teachings made the Nephites happy.
They said, "If Jesus lives after he
dies, then we will too!" They knew
someday they could live with God.

2 Nephi 8-18

WEALTHY NEPHITES

Nephi was getting old. So he gave the brass plates to Jacob. It was Jacob's turn to write about the Nephites. Some of the Nephites were getting wealthy. They had lots of shiny gold and pretty things.

They were not being nice to people
who were poor. The Lord asked
Jacob to talk to the Nephites. So
Jacob told the people to help the
poor, and to feed the hungry, and to
clothe the naked. Jacob said, *"Before
ye seek for riches, seek ye for the
kingdom of God."* Jacob taught them
to be kind to all people.

Jacob 2, (Jacob 2:18)

PRAYERS ARE ANSWERED

The Lord also told Jacob to talk to the Nephites about another problem. Some of the women and children were unhappy. Their husbands and fathers were not following the commandments. Some were not home very much to take care of their families.

The women and children prayed to
Heavenly Father. He heard their
prayers. He saw their sadness. God
asked Jacob to talk to the husbands
and fathers.

So Jacob talked to the men. He said,
"God wants you to obey His
commandments. He wants you to love
and respect your wives. He wants you
to show your children the right way to
live. This will bring happiness."

Jacob 2

THERE IS A CHRIST

A man named Sherem came to
the people of Nephi. He spoke very
well. The people liked listening to
him. Many people followed his
teachings. But he did not teach the
truth. He did not teach about Jesus.

One day he met Jacob. He wanted
Jacob to say there was no Christ. But
Jacob prayed to God. He read the
scriptures. He believed in Christ.

Then Sherem asked Jacob for proof of Christ. Jacob told Sherem that you should not ask God for proof when you already know there is a Christ. But if Sherem really wanted proof, then he would ask God to strike Sherem down.

And God did strike Sherem and he
fell to the ground. Sherem asked
people to come to him. He told them
there really is a Christ. He told them
to listen to Jacob.

Jacob 7

ENOS

When Jacob became old, he gave the brass plates to his son, Enos. It was his turn to write about the Nephites. Enos was a good man.

One day, Enos went hunting in the forest. He decided to pray to Heavenly Father. He knelt down on the ground and prayed in a loud voice. He prayed all day long. Evening came and he was still praying. He asked, "God, please forgive me."

Finally Enos heard a voice. It said,
"Enos, thy sins are forgiven thee, and
thou shalt be blessed." Enos knew
God could not lie so he was very
happy.

Then Enos prayed for his people. He loved them very much. He did not want the Lamanites to destroy them. God answered, "If you have faith, I will protect you."

The Book of Enos (Enos 1:5)

KING BENJAMIN

Many years passed. The brass plates were passed from father to son for many years. When Amaleki did not have a son, he passed the brass plates to King Benjamin. King Benjamin was a good man. He was the son of King Mosiah. King Mosiah had an adventure that he told his son about.

ZARAHEMLA

King Mosiah was warned by the Lord to leave the land of Nephi. King Mosiah and the righteous Nephites were led by the Lord through the wilderness, to the land of Zarahemla. They met some people there. The people were not Nephites. The people were not Lamanites. They called themselves the people of Zarahemla. A long time ago, their ancestors came from Jerusalem.

The people were happy to see the
Nephites. But their language was
different. They could not talk to
each other very well. The people of
Zarahemla wanted to learn the
Nephites' language. Then they could
learn about each other.

The Nephites had the brass plates.
The brass plates told about
Jerusalem. Now the people of
Zarahemla could learn about their
history. They asked King Mosiah to
be their ruler. They lived together in
Zarahemla. They lived in peace.

After a while a small group of Nephites decided to go back to the land of Nephi. Zeniff led them. They wandered in the wilderness until they found the land of Nephi. The land was now owned by the Lamanites. They asked the Lamanite king if they could live there. He let them live in the land of Lehi-Nephi.

The Book of Omni

SIXTEEN STRONG MEN

After many years, King Mosiah's grandson, who was also named Mosiah, became king. The younger king Mosiah sent sixteen strong men from Zarahemla to look for the group of men led by Zeniff. Zeniff left Zarahemla many years before. After forty days of hiking in the wilderness, the sixteen strong men found the land of Lehi-Nephi.

Three of the strongest men walked up to
the city wall. The city guards bound them
and put them in a prison cell for two
days. On the second day, the three men
were allowed to talk to the king of Lehi-
Nephi. His name was King Limhi. Ammon
was one of the strong men. He told King
Limhi that they were from Zarahemla.
They wanted to know what happened to
the small group of Nephites that had left
Zarahemla many years before.

When the king heard this, he was
very happy. He did not know anyone
was looking for them. Now that
Ammon and his strong friends had
found them, they would be able to go
back to Zarahemla. Ammon could
show them the way home.

Mosiah 7

HARDSHIPS IN LEHI-NEPHI

King Limhi told Ammon about the
people of Lehi-Nephi. King Limhi's
grandfather was Zeniff. Zeniff and his
followers found the land of Nephi
after leaving Zarahemla. Zeniff asked
the Lamanite king, Laman, if he could
live there.

The king said, "Yes." He told Zeniff he
could live in the city Lehi-Nephi. Zeniff
and his people worked hard. They
built buildings. They grew food to eat.
They raised sheep for wool to make
clothing. They had what they needed.

When the Lamanites saw all the good
things that Zeniff's people had from
working hard, they wanted it too. But
they did not want to work for it. So
they started taking the Nephites' food
and sheep without asking. And they
started fighting with the hard-working
Nephites. This was a very sad time
for Zeniff and his people.

Mosiah 9-10

KING NOAH

After Zeniff passed away, his son, Noah, began to rule over the people of Lehi-Nephi. He was a mean and selfish king. He did not obey the commandments. He did not remember God. He made his people work hard so he could have nice, fancy things. The people were not happy.

ABINADI

The Lord sent a prophet. His name was Abinadi. He reminded the people to follow God and they did not like that. So city guards took Abinadi to see the wicked King Noah. Abinadi told King Noah to repent. He told him to remember the Lord. But King Noah did not want to change his selfish ways.

He asked his priests to find a reason
to punish Abinadi. His priests asked
Abinadi many questions. Abinadi told
them about Jesus. He told the priests
to repent and teach people the truth.
They were not teaching the truth.

But the priests were angry. They did not want to change. They tried to grab Abinadi. But Abinadi said, *"Touch me not...for I have not delivered the message which the Lord sent me to deliver."* Then the priests were not able to touch Abinadi. The Lord protected him.

Mosiah 13-16 (Mosiah 13:3)

ALMA

After Abinadi finished speaking to the priests, they were angry with him. They did not want to change their selfish ways. They did not want to teach people the truth.

But one of the priests knew Abinadi
was right. He knew God wanted
them to change their ways. His name
was Alma.

Alma asked the priests to let Abinadi go free. But they refused to let him go. Now the priests were angry with Alma too. They wanted to kill both Alma and Abinadi. But Alma fled from the city and was safe from King Noah.

Mosiah 17

THE CHURCH OF CHRIST

Alma hid from King Noah and his mean priests outside of the city. They still wanted to kill him. But quietly, Alma began telling people about Abinadi. He told them of Abinadi's teachings about Jesus. Many people believed in Jesus. They were baptized.

They named their church "The Church
of Christ." After many people joined The
Church of Christ, King Noah heard
where Alma was hiding. He was still
mad at Alma and went looking for him.
But God protected Alma and all of his
followers. They fled into the wilderness.
King Noah did not find them.

Mosiah 18

A NEW KING

Many people did not like King Noah. One day the Lamanites attacked his kingdom. King Noah commanded everyone to leave the city. Most of the people fled into the wilderness. But some angry men in King Noah's kingdom went after King Noah and killed him.

Then, just as the Lamanites were about
to capture the people of Lehi-Nephi,
they had an idea. They gathered their
beautiful daughters together to meet
the Lamanites. Their daughters asked
the Lamanites not to hurt them or their
families. The Lamanite men were
charmed by their beauty. They did not
harm them or their families. They let
them live in their city.

But the Lamanites now took half of
everything they owned. Every year
the people of Lehi-Nephi had to give
the Lamanites half of their food and
belongings. Limhi was King Noah's
son. Now that his father was gone,
he was their new king. King Limhi
and his people were sad. They had
to work very, very hard.

Mosiah 19-21

LAMANITE DAUGHTERS

Before King Noah died, he had many priests. They were mean like King Noah. They were mean to Abinadi and Alma. The priests were mean to other people too. So when the Lamanites started attacking their city, they fled into the wilderness to hide.

The priests knew they could not
return to the city. Angry people might
try to kill them. So the mean priests
lived in the wilderness.

One day, some Lamanite girls were out
in the wilderness, too. They were
singing and dancing and having lots of
fun. The wicked priests saw them.
They decided to take the girls away to
live with them. When the Lamanites
discovered that twenty-four of their
daughters were missing, they became
angry with the people of Limhi.

The Lamanites thought the people of Limhi had kidnapped their daughters. They did not know about the wicked priests. The Lamanites went to war against the people of Limhi. Many people died. The Lamanite king got hurt. The people of Limhi cared for his wounds and took him to King Limhi. King Limhi asked, "Why did you attack us?" The Lamanite king told him about their missing daughters.

King Limhi was surprised. He did not
know anything about their missing
daughters. Gideon reminded them
about the wicked priests hiding in the
wilderness.

The people of Limhi returned the
Lamanite king to his people. When the
Lamanites saw them coming without
weapons, they did not start fighting.
They listened to their king. They
decided it was the wicked priests who
had taken their daughters.

Mosiah 20

KING LIMHI

When Ammon heard King Limhi's stories of hardships, he was sad. The Lamanites made them work very hard. Ammon wanted to help King Limhi. He told him about Jesus. King Limhi was a good man. He and most of his people believed in Jesus and wanted to obey His commandments.

Now that Ammon and his strong
friends had found the lost Nephites,
they needed a way to return them to
Zarahemla. The Lamanites would not
let them go freely. They must think of
a safe way to leave Lehi-Nephi. They
wanted to go home.

Mosiah 22

95

GIDEON'S PLAN

Gideon had a plan to escape. He told everyone to leave the city at night. He said the Lamanites who watched the city gate would be sleeping. King Limhi liked this plan.

All the people gathered their belongings. The Nephites gave the guards something to drink. It made them sleepy. The Nephites quietly left the city during the night. They followed Ammon. After many days, they found Zarahemla. They rejoiced to be in a safe land.

Mosiah 22

A BEAUTIFUL LAND

One time, the mean King Noah chased a good man named Alma and his followers into the wilderness. Alma found a beautiful place with pure water and open land. They began to build a city here. They planted food to eat. They had all that they needed.

They praised God. The people loved
Alma. They asked Alma to be their
king. Alma said, "Let no one rule over
you. Only look to God." They called
their new home Helam.

Mosiah 23

LAMANITES TAKE HELAM

One day while the people of Helam were working in their fields, they saw Lamanite soldiers coming towards them. They were frightened. The Lamanite soldiers looked wild.

The people of Helam ran from their
gardens into the city. Alma tried to
calm them. But the Lamanites came
and took over their land. They were
mean to Alma and the other
Nephites. They made Alma and his
friends work for them.

Alma and his friends prayed to God. The Lamanites told them to stop praying. So now they could only pray in their hearts. God heard their silent prayers, though, and the people felt His love.

Mosiah 24

A DEEP SLEEP

The Lord heard the silent prayers of Alma and his friends. One night He told Alma to leave Helam the next morning. All of the people gathered their flocks and belongings.

In the morning, God made the
Lamanites fall into a deep sleep.
Alma and his friends ran away from
Helam and the sleeping Lamanites.
With God's help, they found
Zarahemla.

They thanked the Lord for bringing them to Zarahemla. King Mosiah and the people of Zarahemla rejoiced. Everyone was very happy.

Mosiah 24

ALMA SEES AN ANGEL

Alma was the High Priest in The Church of Christ. But his son, Alma the younger, and King Mosiah's four sons did not believe in Christ. They told people not to listen to their fathers who taught of Christ.

This made Alma sad. He prayed to God. Many of his friends prayed also. The Lord heard their prayers. He sent an angel to visit Alma's son. Alma the younger and Mosiah's four sons were very frightened when they saw the angel.

First they felt the earth shake under their feet. Then the angel spoke to them. He said, "There is a God and you need to follow His commandments." When the angel left, Alma the younger fell to the ground. For two days his eyes were closed. While his eyes were closed, he asked, "Lord, forgive me for causing so much trouble." Alma the elder prayed that his son would wake up.

After two days, Alma the younger opened his eyes. He said, "Now I know there is a Christ." He felt very bad for all the trouble he had caused. Now he wanted to tell people about Christ. So he became a missionary.

Mosiah 27

ALMA'S MISSION

Alma the younger traveled to many cities as a missionary. He told lots of people about Jesus. Many people were happy to meet Alma. They wanted to join the church of Christ. But in one city, people would not listen. They told Alma to leave.

After leaving the city, an angel
appeared to Alma. He told Alma to
return to the city to teach the people.
Alma fasted and prayed before going
back. He returned to the city through
a different gate.

He was very hungry from fasting. He
saw a man and asked him for food.
The man invited Alma to his house to
eat and they became good friends.

Alma 8, 10

AMULEK

Alma's new friend was Amulek. He was popular in his city. He had many friends. He had lots of nice things, too. But before he met Alma he did not understand the teachings of Jesus. Amulek told this story of how he met Alma.

One day while Amulek was going to
see a friend in his city, an angel
stopped him. The angel told Amulek
to return to his home. The angel
wanted him to give food to a holy
man. Amulek did not know who the
holy man would be, but he did what
the angel asked him to do.

On the way home, he met a man.
The man asked Amulek for food.
Amulek knew this must be the holy
man the angel wanted him to feed.
He brought the man back to his
home and gave him food.

The man's name was Alma. They
became very good friends. Amulek
believed Alma's teachings of Jesus
and he and Alma became missionary
companions. They traveled all over
the land telling people about Jesus.

Alma 10

116

MEETING ZEEZROM

In one city, Alma and Amulek met a man. His name was Zeezrom. Zeezrom told Amulek that he would give him lots of money if he would say there is no God. Amulek was surprised. He said, "I know there is a God. And you know it too!"

Amulek taught Zeezrom many things about God. Then Zeezrom knew what he did was wrong. He should not have offered money to Amulek to say there is not a God. Zeezrom was frightened now and his body started shaking.

Some people that were watching were angry with Amulek. They liked Zeezrom and they did not want to believe in Christ. The people watching wanted to hurt Amulek. But Zeezrom asked them not to hurt him. He said, "Amulek is right. There is a God." But the people put Amulek and Alma in prison anyway.

Alma 14

ALMA AND AMULEK IN PRISON

Everyday people came to see Amulek and Alma in prison. The people who came to visit were mean and cruel to them. They did not like them because they believed in Jesus. Sometimes they also hurt other people who believed in Jesus.

After twelve days in prison, Alma and Amulek got very tired of being hit, yelled at and called bad names. Alma and Amulek really wanted to leave the prison. Feeling frustrated, Alma stood up in the prison cell and cried out in a loud voice to God. He asked, *"How long shall we suffer these great afflictions, O Lord?"* The Lord was watching over them. He heard Alma's prayer.

God caused the earth to shake. The
prison walls fell to the ground.
Everyone in the prison died except
Alma and Amulek. They were fine
now. They walked away from the
fallen prison unharmed. People outside
the prison were frightened when they
saw Alma and Amulek. They knew
God's power had freed them.

All the people in the city ran away!
After hurting Alma and Amulek in
prison they were afraid God might be
angry and hurt them back. But Alma
and Amulek did not want to hurt
anyone. They just wanted to tell
people about Jesus. They left the city.

Alma 14, (Alma 14:26)

ZEEZROM IS HEALED

Alma and Amulek left Zeezrom's city and walked to the next city. Here, the people were happy to see Alma and Amulek and they welcomed them.

Their new friend, Zeezrom, was in
the city. He was feeling very sick
and needed to stay in bed. He sent
a message asking Alma and Amulek
to come visit him. Zeezrom was
very happy when they came to see
him. He told them he was sorry for
causing so much trouble.

Then Zeezrom asked them if they
could heal him from his sickness.
Alma asked Zeezrom if he believed in
Christ? Zeezrom said, "Yes, I believe
everything you have taught me."
Then Alma told him, "If you believe in
Christ, then you can be healed."

Then Alma blessed him. When Alma
finished the blessing, Zeezrom jumped
out of bed! He could walk now. He
was healed! Zeezrom asked to be
baptized. He joined Christ's church.
Then he, too, became a missionary.

Alma 15

THE SCATTERED SHEEP

Mosiah's four sons also became missionaries. They decided to teach the Lamanites about Jesus. One of Mosiah's sons was named Ammon. Ammon became a servant to the mean king of the Lamanites. His name was King Lamoni.

Ammon wanted to work for King
Lamoni so he could tell him about
Jesus. One day Ammon was watching
the king's sheep. While Ammon was
taking the sheep to get a drink from a
watering hole, some mean men
stopped them. The mean men made
the sheep run away.

Some of King Lamoni's servants who
were with Ammon, started crying.
Other servants who lost the king's
sheep before were put to death for
losing them. They thought the king
might kill them too. But Ammon said,
"Let's go and gather the sheep." With
much work, they gathered all the
sheep. But again when they arrived
at the watering hole, the mean men
started scattering the sheep.

The sheep ran away again. Ammon
and the other servants gathered the
sheep for a second time. The sheep
needed a drink so they took them
back to the watering hole. But the
mean men scared off the sheep
again. This happened three times!

Alma 17

AMMON'S GREAT STRENGTH

After gathering the sheep for the third time, Ammon asked the servants to watch the sheep. He said he would take care of the mean men.

While walking towards the group of
mean men, Ammon picked up some
rocks. He started throwing the rocks
at the men. Each man that he hit fell
to the ground. The mean men tried to
hit Ammon back. But they could not
hit Ammon.

This made them very angry. They started running towards Ammon with clubs. But Ammon cut off the arm of every man who lifted a club to kill him. There were many men coming against Ammon. But God gave him great strength. The men were surprised that Ammon was so strong. When the men saw his great strength, they ran away quickly.

Alma 17

KING LAMONI'S CONVERSION

The servants of King Lamoni were shocked. How could Ammon scare away all the mean men by himself? The servants told the king what happened. The king was amazed. The king thought Ammon must be a great spirit.

When Ammon came to see the king, the king was speechless. He did not know what to say to Ammon. But with God's help, Ammon could read King Lamoni's silent thoughts. He answered all of the king's questions.

Then Ammon told the king about God. King Lamoni believed all his words. Once he believed in God, he felt terrible for all the mean things he had done. He cried out to God asking for mercy.

Then he fell to the ground. He was taken to his wife and was laid on a bed. His wife and children were sad to see him this way. After two days and two nights, the queen asked to see Ammon.

She asked Ammon if her husband was still alive. Some of her servants thought the king was dead. But the queen thought he was still alive. Ammon went to King Lamoni. Ammon knew the king was just sleeping. He was learning about Jesus. Ammon told the queen that Lamoni would wake up the next day. She had faith that this was going to happen.

Alma 18-19

ABISH

On the third day, King Lamoni
awoke from his sleep. The queen
was so happy to see him awake!
King Lamoni told her all about Jesus.
He got so excited telling her that he
fell to the ground again. The queen
got so excited that she fell to the
ground, too. Ammon and the other
servants in the room fell down also!

They all looked like they were dead,
lying on the floor. One woman servant
was awake. Her name was Abish.
She wanted to tell the Lamanites
about King Lamoni. She hoped
everyone would believe in Jesus.
Some of the people did believe, but
some did not.

One man, who did not believe in Jesus, saw Ammon lying on the floor. Ammon had cut off his brother's arm at the watering hole. So this man wanted to kill Ammon for what he did to his brother. The man raised his sword to kill Ammon, but God protected Ammon. The man fell to the ground and died.

Ammon was still dreaming about
Jesus. Seeing how confused all of the
people were, Abish went to the
queen. She touched her hand to
wake her. The queen awoke and
stood up. She was so happy, she
said many things about Jesus.

Then she touched the king's hand. He awoke and stood up. The king told the Lamanites about Jesus. Most of the people in his kingdom believed also. They praised God. They lived in peace.

Alma 18-19

A PEACEFUL PEOPLE

When the Lamanites learned about God, they were filled with love. They joined Christ's church. They wanted to help each other. They did not want to hurt or kill people anymore, so they buried all of their weapons deep in the ground.

Some Lamanites from another city
came to fight them. But the new
converts would not fight back. They
promised to never fight again. The
Lamanites were surprised when
they came to fight. The converts did
not have any weapons. And they
would not fight back. They only
praised God.

At first, many converts died because they would not fight back. But soon some Lamanites started putting down their weapons. They would not fight either. They joined the converts. They believed in God. They lived in peace.

Alma 24

KING OVER ALL THE LAMANITES

King Lamoni was so happy to learn about Jesus that he wanted to tell his father about Him. His father was king over all the Lamanites. He asked Ammon to come with him to meet his father. But God told Ammon not to go. He said his brothers were in prison in Middoni. He wanted Ammon to go help them.

King Lamoni was a friend of the king
in Middoni. He asked if he could go
with Ammon to help him. They went
together. While traveling, they met
Lamoni's father. His father asked
them where they were going. Lamoni
was excited to tell him about
Ammon. He told him they were going
to Middoni to help Ammon's brothers.

Lamoni was surprised to see his father getting angry. Lamoni's father did not want his son to help a Nephite, like Ammon. He told his son to slay Ammon. But Lamoni refused to hurt Ammon.

Then Lamoni's father took out a
sword to slay his son. Ammon
stopped him. He did not want anyone
to get hurt. Then Lamoni's father said,
"I should not be mad at my son, I
should be mad at you!"

Then the king started attacking
Ammon. Ammon was not hurt. But
the king's arm got hurt and he could
not use it anymore. When the king
saw that Ammon could kill him, he
pled for his life.

Ammon did not want to hurt the king, so instead he asked for three wishes. First, he asked the king to let his brothers go free in Middoni. Then he asked the king to let his son, Lamoni, keep his kingdom. And finally, he asked the king not to be mad at his son anymore. The king was happy to hear that Ammon did not want to slay him.

He granted Ammon all his wishes.
He was impressed that Ammon
cared so much for his son. He asked
Ammon and his brothers to come
teach him about Jesus.

Alma 20

A NEW CONVERT

Ammon went to a new city to do missionary work. His brother, Aaron, stayed with King Lamoni's father to teach him about God. The king believed Aaron's words. The king prayed to God. He asked God to forgive him for all the bad things he had done.

After praying, the king was struck and fell to the ground. A servant ran to the queen and told her what happened. She went to her husband and found him lying on the ground. Aaron and his brothers were standing over the king. It looked like they had caused him to fall.

The queen ordered the servants to slay Aaron. But the servants were afraid to touch him. They knew he had great power. When the queen saw how frightened they were, she asked them to gather people from her kingdom to slay Aaron.

But Aaron did not want to die. So he walked over to the king and put out his hand to raise him. The king awoke and stood up. He told his people about Jesus. Many of them believed his words and joined The Church of Christ.

Alma 22

ANTI-NEPHI-LEHIES

After the King of the Lamanites joined the church, he taught many people about Jesus. Lots of Lamanites joined The Church of Christ. Ammon, Aaron and their other brothers were hard at work telling people about Jesus. This was a very happy time for the missionaries.

Lamanites in seven cities believed in
Jesus now. They called themselves the
Anti-Nephi-Lehies. They were friendly
to the Nephites. The Anti-Nephi-Lehies
all buried their weapons and promised
to never fight again.

Alma 24

GOD LIVES!

Alma the younger was a high priest in Zarahemla. When people did bad things they were brought to Alma. He would decide on their punishment.

One day, a man named Korihor was brought to Alma. Korihor did not believe in God. He taught others not to believe in God, too. People in Zarahemla could choose what they wanted to believe. But Korihor was causing so much trouble in Zarahemla, that the people asked Alma to talk to him.

Alma asked Korihor, "Why do you not believe in God?" Korihor said, "Because there is no proof that God lives." Korihor asked Alma for proof of God. Alma said, "We have lots of proof."

"We have scriptures that tell us about
God. We have prophets who tell us
about God. Our earth and everything
on it shows us God's greatness. All
the planets which move in patterns
show us God's greatness. All these
things show us that God lives!"

Alma 30

KORIHOR LOSES HIS VOICE

Korihor asked Alma again for proof. Alma said, "I'm sorry you do not believe in God. If you want proof I will ask God to take away your voice. Then you will know God lives and you will not be able to cause any more trouble." Korihor said, "Give me proof or I will not stop causing trouble!"

Then God took away Korihor's voice. The people watching were surprised. They asked Korihor to write about losing his voice. Korihor wrote, "I do believe in God. Only God has the power to take away my voice."

"I should not have followed the devil's beliefs. I caused a lot of trouble. The devil will not help me now. I should have followed God's word instead. Heavenly Father helps righteous people."

Alma 30

MISSIONARY WORK

Alma decided to go to a land called Antionum. He took other missionaries with him. They heard that the people needed help. The people were forgetting about God. They were replacing the true God with a different one.

When Alma and his friends came to a synagogue, they went inside to talk to the people. But they were shocked by what they saw. They had never seen people worshiping this way. They worshiped on a high stand. Each person said the exact same prayer.

Then during the week, they never thought about God. They were dressed in gold and silver and beautiful clothes. They thought they were better than other people because of their nice clothes. They were even mean to people who did not have gold and silver and nice things.

They would not allow poor people to
enter their synagogues either. Alma
and his friends taught the people
about the true God. Alma said, "We
can pray to God anywhere, not just
from a high stand. And we should
pray often, not just once a week. And
we should have faith in God."

Alma said, *"...if ye have faith ye hope for things which are not seen, which are true."* Many of the people, who did not have gold and silver and nice clothes, had faith in God. They believed Alma's words.

Alma 31-35, (Alma 32:21)

CAPTAIN MORONI

After several years, the Lamanites
started fighting with the Nephites. The
Lamanites did not like the Nephites
and they did not believe in God. The
Nephites wanted to protect their
homes and families. They wanted to
worship God.

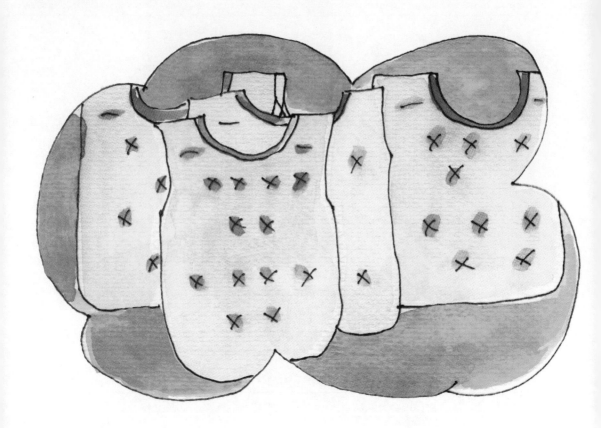

The Nephites chose a man named Moroni to lead their army. He was a smart man. He asked his soldiers to make and wear metal breast plates to protect their bodies. He also sent secret spies to find out when and where the Lamanites were planning to attack. Because of this, the Nephites were prepared.

When the Lamanites attacked, they had twice as many soldiers as the Nephites. But because Captain Moroni was a smart and courageous leader, the Nephites won this battle.

Alma 43-44

TITLE OF LIBERTY

Amalickiah was a large and wicked man. He really wanted to be king over the Nephites. He started causing lots of problems among the people. He wanted the Nephites to stop believing in Christ and to follow him. When Captain Moroni learned of Amalickiah's plan he became angry! Captain Moroni did not want the Nephites to stop believing in God. He knew God blessed and protected them.

In memory of our God, our religion, and freedom, and our people, our wives, and our children -

Captain Moroni tore off his coat. On it he wrote a Title of Liberty for all the Nephites to see. In a loud voice he called to the Nephites and marched through the land to gather an army. The people came running and rallied with Captain Moroni. They tore off some of their clothing and put it at Moroni's feet. They made a special promise to remember and follow God.

These Nephites were true believers in Christ and were called Christians. Amalickiah was not very popular with the Nephites now, so he and his followers left to join the Lamanites. Captain Moroni placed the Title of Liberty on every tower in the land. This would remind the Nephites of their new covenant.

Alma 46:12

HELAMAN

The Lamanites kept losing many battles. But they still continued to fight. They really wanted power over the Nephites. There were not as many Nephite soldiers as the Lamanites. The Nephites did not know what to do. They needed more soldiers.

The people of Ammon felt sad and
helpless. They had buried their
weapons in the ground and
promised God that they would never
fight again. But now they wanted to
help the Nephites protect their
homes. Helaman said, "You made a
promise to God that you would not
fight anymore, so you should keep
your promise. We understand.
Please do not feel sad. God will
bless us because of your promise."

The people of Ammon told Helaman
that their young sons did not make
this promise, so they could be his
soldiers. Helaman counted their
young sons. There were two
thousand strong boys. They would
be of tremendous help to the
Nephites. Helaman called his new
soldiers his stripling warriors.

Alma 53

THE STRIPLING WARRIORS

Helaman and the two thousand stripling warriors went to help protect a Nephite city. Helaman had a plan. He and his two thousand stripling warriors would march away from the city. Lamanite soldiers would want to follow them. Soon other Nephite soldiers would start following behind the Lamanites.

After three days of marching in the
wilderness, the Nephites circled
around the Lamanites. There was a
big battle. Helaman was very worried
about his young soldiers. His stripling
warriors had never fought in a battle
before. But they were fearless. They
told Helaman that their mothers
taught them that if they did not fear,
God would protect them.

After winning the fierce battle, Helaman counted his young warriors. Many people died. He thought some of his young warriors might have died too. But when he counted them, they were all alive! His stripling warriors believed in God and He protected them. God gave them great strength and courage.

Alma 56

SAMUEL THE LAMANITE

Many years passed. The Lamanites became righteous. They believed in God. They followed His commandments. But now only a few Nephites were righteous. Heavenly Father was not happy. He sent a Lamanite prophet to talk to the Nephites. His name was Samuel.

The Nephites did not like hearing Samuel's words. They decided to throw him out of their city. But the Lord told Samuel to go back. He wanted the Nephites to hear his words. They needed to know that Jesus would be born soon. When Samuel returned to the city, the Nephites would not let him come in. So Samuel climbed the city wall. From the top of the wall, he told the people many things in a loud voice.

Some people believed him. They
joined Christ's church. But some
people did not believe him. They
started throwing stones at him and
shooting arrows. The Lord protected
Samuel. Not one arrow or stone hit
him. When the Nephites saw that
God was protecting him, even more
people believed Samuel's words.

Those who did not believe Samuel, started chasing him and tried to catch him. But Samuel ran from them and went home to his fellow Lamanites. He accomplished what the Lord asked him to do.

Helaman 13-16

THE GADIANTON ROBBERS

The righteous Nephites and the righteous Lamanites joined together. Because the Lamanites were righteous, their skin became fair and they called themselves Nephites.

Lachoneous was their ruler. He
received a letter from a bad group
named the Gadianton robbers. They
asked Lachoneous to let them rule
over the Nephites. Lachoneous was
surprised. The Gadianton robbers did
mean and terrible things.

Lachoneous and his people wanted to follow God. Lachoneous was not afraid of the Gadianton robbers. He only feared God. He made a plan to protect his people from the Gadianton robbers.

3 Nephi 2-3

REMEMBER GOD

Lachoneous and all the Nephites moved into two cities. They brought their families and sheep and food. They made weapons. They were preparing to protect themselves from the Gadianton robbers.

Lachoneous told his people the most
important thing to do is to remember
God, to pray to God and to follow His
commandments. This would save
them from the Gadianton robbers.

3 Nephi 4

PRAYING FOR STRENGTH

One day, the Nephites saw the Gadianton robbers running towards their city to fight them. There were many Gadianton robbers. They looked mean and scary. Their skin and clothing were dyed bright red.

When the Gadianton robbers came,
the Nephites fell to the ground. The
Gadianton robbers were happy. They
thought the Nephites were frightened
by their ugly appearance. But the
Nephites only feared God. They were
praying for strength. There was a
huge battle.

NEPHITES PRAISE GOD

There was a huge battle. The Gadianton robbers attacked the Nephites. It was the largest battle since Lehi came to the Promised Land. Many people died. But the Nephites gained great strength from the Lord and they won the battle.

The Nephites were so happy after the battle that many were singing and dancing. Many were even crying. They were so happy that God had saved them from the Gadianton robbers. They sang to God, *"Hosanna to the Most High God...Blessed be the name of the Lord God Almighty, the Most High God."*

3 Nephi 4, (3 Nephi 4:32)

THE SIGN

Many prophets had lived in the promised land now. Many of them had the same message. Like Samuel the Lamanite, they had told the people that Jesus was coming to live on the earth soon. They told the people a sign would be given.

The sign was that a new star would
appear in the sky. Also a day would
end but it would still be light outside.
All night long it would be light. Then in
the morning the sun would rise again.
The righteous people were looking for
this sign. They were happy that Jesus
would be born soon.

3 Nephi 1

UNBELIEVERS

There were many people who believed Jesus would be born soon. They were looking for the new star to appear and for the night that would stay light. But there were some unbelievers. They were mean to the people who believed. The unbelievers said the time was past for Jesus to come. They told the believers that their beliefs were in vain.

This made the believers feel unhappy.
But they still thought Jesus would
come. The unbelievers were so mean
they even set a date to kill the
believers. They said if the sign did not
appear by that date, then they would
kill all of the believers.

3 Nephi 1

NEPHI

Helaman's grandson was Nephi.
Nephi was keeping the brass plates
now. He was very sad about the
unbelievers. He prayed to God. Nephi
did not want any harm to come to
the believers.

Then God answered his prayers. He told Nephi not to worry. Jesus would be born the next day and the sign would appear.

3 Nephi 1

JESUS IS BORN

The next evening, the sun set. But the sky did not turn dark. The people were surprised. It stayed light all night. Then they saw a beautiful new star in the sky. In the morning, the sun rose.

The unbelievers were astonished.
This was exactly how the prophets
had said it would happen. People
who believed in Jesus were very,
very happy. They knew this was the
sign from God. Jesus was born!

3 Nephi 1

STORMS AND DARKNESS

The prophets told of another sign. They said that when Jesus died, there would be great storms. The earth would shake, too. Then there would be three days and three nights of darkness. After the third night, the sun would finally rise. And Jesus would rise also. He would live again.

The prophets were right. The sign came just as they said it would. There was a huge storm and the earth shook. Then for three days and three nights, the sky was completely dark.

3 Nephi 8

JESUS' VISIT

One day the people gathered together near a temple. They were talking about Jesus. What did it mean that Jesus would die, but live again? While talking, they heard a soft, piercing voice. They looked toward heaven.

They heard a voice say, *"Behold My Beloved Son, in whom I am well pleased, in whom I have glorified my name—hear ye him."* Then they saw a man wearing a white robe descending out of heaven.

The people thought it was an angel. But he stretched forth his hands and said, *"Behold, I am Jesus Christ, whom the prophets testified shall come into the world."* All of the people watching fell to the ground. They remembered the prophets saying Jesus would visit them. They felt His love and felt very special.

3 Nephi 11 (3 Nephi 11:7 & 10)

JESUS' TEACHINGS

Jesus stayed with them and taught them many things. He said, "You need to follow the commandments. You should also be baptized and receive the Holy Ghost. You should be nice to each other, too. You should try not to be angry. We will all live in heaven if we do these things."

The people were filled with love.
They did not want Jesus to leave.
Jesus said, "I will stay with you a little
longer and bless the sick."

People who were sick, lame, blind
and dumb came to Jesus. He healed
each one of them. Everyone bowed
down to Jesus. They worshiped Him.
They felt so much love from Him.

3 Nephi 17

JESUS AND THE CHILDREN

Jesus asked the little children to come to Him. He waited for each child to come. Not one child was left out. Each child was important to Jesus.

When all the children were together,
Jesus asked them to kneel. He taught
the children how to pray. He prayed
to our Father in Heaven. The children
and Jesus felt so happy. Jesus loved
the children so much, he even cried.

He took each child one by one and prayed for them and blessed them. The heavens were opened and angels came down and circled around the children. The angels taught the children important things. It was a wonderful day for the little children.

3 Nephi 17

PEACE ON EARTH

When Jesus visited the Nephites
and Lamanites, He established His
church. Everyone joined. Jesus asked
twelve men to be disciples. They
would teach the people about God
and His church after Jesus left.

Jesus' visit had a great effect on the people. They all wanted to be like Jesus. They wanted to return to Heavenly Father. They always prayed and followed the commandments. Because they followed Jesus' teachings, they all lived together in peace. For two hundred years, they had continual peace.

4 Nephi 1

CORRECT PRAYERS

When Jesus visited the Nephites and Lamanites, He taught them important things. He taught them how to baptize and how to give the Holy Ghost to new members of His church. He taught the correct sacrament prayers for blessing the bread and water.

He also taught the priesthood prayer
to ordain teachers and priests. The
prophet Moroni wrote these prayers
on the brass plates for us. We use
them now just as Jesus taught them.

Moroni 2-6

MORMON

After Jesus left, there were two hundred years of peace. But then some of the people started doing bad things. People started forgetting about Jesus and His church. Both the Nephites and the Lamanites became wicked. Then they started fighting with each other. Finally there were only two Nephites left who believed in Jesus. They were Mormon and his son, Moroni.

Mormon was a large, strong man. He led the Nephites in many battles. But the Nephites no longer believed in Jesus. There were many Lamanites who wanted to destroy the Nephites. Mormon had the brass plates. He wrote many important things on them. Then he gave some of them to his son, Moroni.

LITTLE CHILDREN ARE SPECIAL

Before giving the brass plates to
Moroni, Mormon wrote a letter to his
son. He wrote about little children.
Moroni wanted to know if babies and
young children should be baptized.
So Mormon prayed to God to find out.

The Lord told Mormon that babies
were born pure and sinless. They did
not need to be baptized until they were
older. Children must be able to repent
of their sins before they are baptized.
Babies and little children are not able
to repent yet. Moroni was happy to
learn this. Now he knew that all babies
were born pure and did not need to be
baptized until they were older. He
learned that all children are special.

Moroni 8

FAITH, HOPE AND CHARITY

Moroni was all alone after his father, Mormon, passed away. The Lamanites and Nephites were all wicked now. No one remembered God. Moroni was the only righteous person left. The Lord spoke to Moroni.

He showed Moroni the future. Moroni
saw a busy, changing world. He saw
people who liked money a lot. They
liked the things money could buy
more than they liked helping poor
and needy people.

Moroni saw only a few people who helped the poor and needy. These people remembered God. They wanted to be like Jesus. These people had faith, hope and charity. Charity is the pure love of Christ. Heavenly Father and Jesus want all people to have this love.

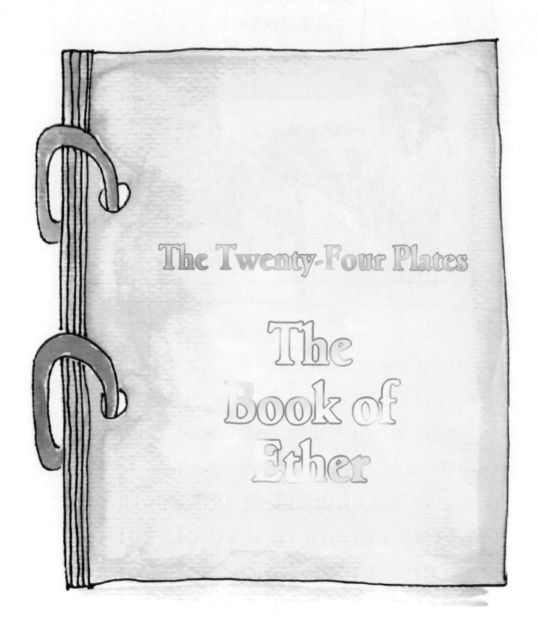

The Twenty-Four Plates

The Book of Ether

FINDING THE PLATES

When Limhi was king of the city Lehi-Nephi, he sent men to find the city of Zarahemla. But they did not find it. Instead the men found an old, desolate city. Nobody lived there anymore.

The men wondered what happened
to the people who used to live in the
city. They found twenty-four plates
with writing on them. They thought
the plates would tell about the
people who used to live there. They
brought the plates back to King Limhi
to read. But when he could not read
the writings, he kept the plates for a
long time.

Then, when King Limhi and his
people finally returned to Zarahemla,
he showed the plates to King Mosiah.
King Mosiah said he could read the
twenty-four plates. He said the plates
were called the Book of Ether.

Ether 1, Mosiah 22

THE BOOK OF ETHER

Long, long ago some people
started building a very tall tower to
stand on. They wanted it to reach
heaven so they could be closer to
God. But in the Book of Ether, we learn
this is not how we get closer to God.
We get closer by praying everyday and
by studying the scriptures.

God did not want the people to build a
tower to reach heaven. So He caused
a big earthquake and the tower fell to
the ground. Then He gave everyone a
different language. If the people could
not communicate, it would be difficult
to build another tower.

Ether 1

THE BROTHER OF JARED

A man named Jared asked his righteous brother to pray to God. Jared wanted him to ask God if they could keep the same language. They wanted to communicate with each other and with their friends.

Jared's brother prayed to Heavenly
Father. He asked if they could keep
the same language and also asked if
they should leave their city. God was
pleased with Jared and his brother.
They followed His commandments.
Because they were righteous, God let
them have the same language. Then
he told them to gather their families
and friends and leave the city.

Ether 1

FAITH MOVES MOUNTAINS

The brother of Jared had great faith. He had not seen God but he knew God existed. He knew that God heard his prayers. And God always answered his prayers. One day while traveling through a wilderness, the brother of Jared and his family and friends came to a big mountain. They called it Mount Zerin.

Mount Zerin was in their way. They
could not walk over it. The brother of
Jared prayed and asked God to move
the mountain out of their way.
Because the brother of Jared had
faith that God could do this, the
mountain moved out of their way!

Ether 12

EIGHT SMALL BARGES

Jared and his family and friends traveled in the wilderness. They came to a sea. The Lord told them to build boats to cross the sea. They were going to a choice land.

So they built eight small boats. When
they finished building them, they
were tight, like a submarine. Water
from the sea would not come in the
boats. But they had a problem. They
would not have fresh air to breath
since the boats had a top on them.

The Lord told them to put a hole in the top and bottom of each boat. Then when they needed air they could open up the hole. When the sea was stormy, they could close the holes to keep the water out.

Ether 2

LOOKING FOR LIGHT

The eight boats were ready to go, but they were dark inside. The brother of Jared asked God what to do. Instead of telling him what to do, God asked him to think about a solution.

He thought about building a fire in the
boat for light, but a fire would burn a
hole in the boat. Then the boat would
sink. So Jared's brother decided with
God's help he could make light from
shiny stones.

Ether 3

BRIGHT STONES

The brother of Jared cut sixteen clear stones from a rock. Then he prayed to God. He asked God to touch each stone and make them shine bright like a light.

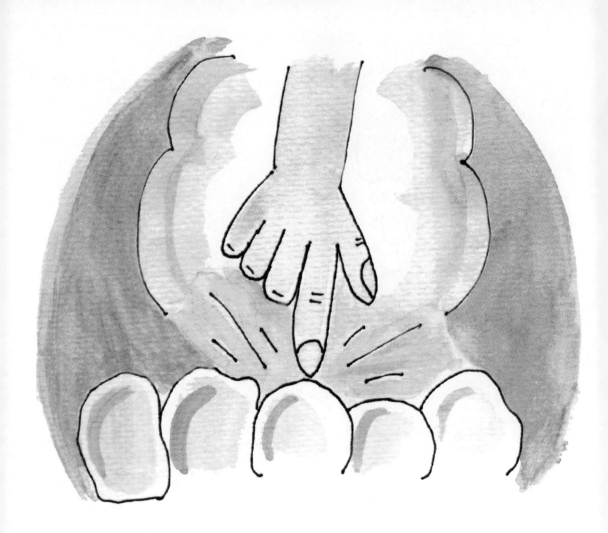

After asking the Lord to do this, he
saw a finger reach out. It touched
each rock. The rocks lit up bright
white! The shining lights lit the inside
of each of the boats.

Ether 3

IMAGE OF GOD

When the brother of Jared saw a finger touch the stones, he was surprised. He fell to the ground. The Lord asked him why he had fallen. The brother of Jared said he did not know that God had a physical body, like a man.

The Lord said, "Because of your faith, you could see me." Then Jesus showed all of himself to the brother of Jared. He said, *"Behold, I am Jesus Christ...all men were created in the beginning after mine own image."*

A CHOICE LAND

The brother of Jared put two bright stones in each boat. This gave plenty of light. The eight boats moved swiftly through the sea. A strong wind pushed them towards the choice land. Sometimes the boats were completely covered with big waves. But the people were safe inside, the boats were tight. Water could not enter the boats.

After many days of traveling, they
came to their new home. They were
excited and grateful to find their new
home. They thanked the Lord for
bringing them to this new land.

Ether 3-6

REMEMBER ME

Jared and his family and friends liked their new home. They planted crops for food. They grew lots of delicious fruits and vegetables. They had food and clothing and all that they needed. They thanked the Lord for all of their blessings. Heavenly Father is very happy when we thank Him for our blessings.

Ether 6

THE LORD'S PROMISE

The Lord told the Jaredites that, "As long as you obey my commandments, you will be happy. You will feel peace and you will have what you need. If you disobey, I cannot promise you happiness."

"But if you are lost, I will send prophets. They will remind you about God. They will ask you to repent. If you follow my words, I will give you happiness and peace. You will feel my love."

Ether 6

MORONI'S PROMISE

Moroni asked people who read the Book of Mormon to think about the stories. Then you should ask Heavenly Father, in the name of Christ, if these stories really happened. If you have faith and really want to know, the Holy Ghost will tell you they are true. He will give you a good feeling inside.

Moroni 10

MORONI HIDES THE PLATES

When Mormon was alive, he had many plates. Some were from Jerusalem where Nephi took them from King Laban and brought them to the Promised Land. Some were from the Jaredites. And some were histories of the Nephites and Lamanites. The plates had been passed down from father to son for many, many years.

Mormon's plates had lots of stories that happened in the promised land. They told about prophets and missionaries and wars and queens and kings. Mormon took the most important parts of the records and put them into one book, made of gold plates. Mormon wanted the records to be safe. If the Lamanites got the records they would destroy them.

So Mormon hid the sacred records in a hill. The hill was called Cumorah. He gave the gold plates to his son, Moroni. Mormon knew that the Lord wanted to save the records for later generations. He wanted people in the latter days to hear these special stories. Moroni added a few things to his father's book, then he buried them in the Hill Cumorah.

Mormon 6

JOSEPH SMITH

Many years after Moroni hid the plates, a young man named Joseph Smith was born. He lived with his family in America. He had three sisters and four living brothers. In his hometown of Manchester in New York State, there were many churches.

His mother and two brothers and one sister attended one church, and his father and other brothers attended a different church. Each Sunday, the preachers called out to people asking them to come join their church. The preachers each said all the other churches were wrong.

Joseph Smith was fourteen years old.
He was very confused about which
church to join. Sometimes he went to
church with his mother and other
times he went with his father.

One day, he was reading from the Bible. It said, *"If any of you lack wisdom, let him ask of God, that giveth to all men liberally, and upbraideth not; and it shall be given him."* Joseph thought about this scripture. To him, this meant that if he prayed about which church to join and had faith in God, then God would tell him which church to join. So Joseph decided to pray to God and ask which church he should join.

Joseph Smith-History (James 1:5)

JOSEPH'S VISION

When Joseph decided to pray to God to ask which church he should join, he walked outside into a quiet grove of trees. He had lots of privacy there. Joseph knelt down and started praying. But he felt strange. He could not see around him and he had a difficult time talking, too. Then suddenly the darkness left and Joseph could talk. He felt much better.

Then he saw two personages coming out of heaven towards him. One said, *"This is My Beloved Son. Hear Him!"* Joseph asked Jesus which church he should join. Jesus told Joseph not to join any of the churches. Jesus said that people had changed the true teachings since Jesus lived on the earth and that He wanted Joseph to restore the true gospel of Jesus Christ.

Later on, an angel named Moroni appeared to Joseph while he was lying in bed. The angel told Joseph where some special golden plates were hidden in a hill. Someday Joseph would get them and translate them. The angel said that the plates contained the histories of people who lived in America a long time ago.

Joseph was surprised! He did not expect to see a vision of Heavenly Father and Jesus Christ. And he did not expect the angel Moroni to visit him either. But his prayers were answered. Now Joseph knew not to join any church, but to start a new one. And he knew Heavenly Father wanted him to get the sacred records that Moroni hid in the Hill Cumorah a long, long time ago. When Joseph translated the golden plates, he called them The Book of Mormon.

Joseph Smith-History, (Joseph Smith-History 1:17)

About the
Author / Illustrator

Laura Lee Blocher Rostrom is a native of Seattle, Washington and is a graduate of Brigham Young University. She has spent most of her adult life living and traveling outside of the United States. She now resides in Tokyo, Japan with her husband, Dean, and their three children.

We hope you enjoy My Book of Mormon Storybook
for many years! To order a copy for a friend, child,
or grandchild please contact CFI (Cedar Fort, Inc.)
at any of the following:

phone: 1-800-SKY-BOOK (759-2665)

facsimile: 1-800-489-9432

e-mail: skybook@itsnet.com